Milly the Meerkat

Written by Oakley Graham

Licensed exclusively to Top That Publishing Ltd
Tide Mill Way, Woodbridge, Suffolk, IP12 1AP, UK
www.topthatpublishing.com
Copyright © 2014 Tide Mill Media
All rights reserved
2 4 6 8 9 7 5 3
Printed and bound in China

Illustrated by Alexia Orkrania
Written by Oakley Graham

ISBN 978-1-84956-753-4

A catalogue record for this book is available from the British Library

For Noah

There once was a young meerkat called Milly, who was bored as she sat on an earth mound taking her turn as lookout.

To amuse herself, Milly took a great, big breath and barked out, 'Snake! Snake! A snake is approaching the baby meerkats' burrow!'

All the other meerkats came running out of their own burrows to help Milly drive the snake away.

But when they arrived at the top of the mound, they found no snake. Milly laughed at the sight of their angry faces.

'Don't bark "snake", Milly,'
said the other meerkats,
'if there's no snake!'

Later that day, Milly was feeling even more bored and barked out again, 'Snake! Snake! A snake is approaching the baby meerkats' burrow!'

To her mischievous delight, Milly watched as the other meerkats rushed to the mound to help her drive the snake away.

But when the other meerkats arrived at the top of the mound, they found no snake. Again, Milly laughed at the sight of their angry faces. 'Don't bark "snake", Milly,' repeated the other meerkats, 'if there's no snake!'

Late in the afternoon,
Milly saw a real
snake slithering
close to the baby
meerkats' burrow.

Alarmed, Milly leapt to her feet and barked out as loudly as she could, 'Snake! Snake! A snake is approaching the baby meerkats' burrow!'

But the other meerkats just thought that Milly was trying to fool them again, so they didn't come out to help her.

Outside, as day turned to night, everyone wondered why Milly hadn't returned for supper. They went to look for Milly and found her crying on top of the lookout mound.

'There really was a snake here! The meerkat babies have scattered! I barked out, "snake" as loudly as I could,' sobbed Milly. 'Why didn't you come to help me?'

A wise, old meerkat tried to comfort Milly
as they walked back to the village.
'We'll help you look for the lost meerkat babies,'
he said, putting his arm around Milly.

'You have learnt an important lesson today, Milly.
Nobody believes a liar ... even when they are
telling the truth!'

The entire meerkat colony helped Milly look for the lost babies and once they were all found, they tucked them up safely in their burrows.

Milly was very sorry for what she had done and promised that she would never lie to her family and friends again.